Willbee the Bumblebee

Story by

Craig Smith & Maureen Thomson

Music by

Illustrated by

Craig Smith   Katz Cowley

SCHOLASTIC

AUCKLAND SYDNEY NEW YORK LONDON TORONTO

MEXICO CITY NEW DELHI HONG KONG

Dedicated to William (Willbee) John Thomson. For his cuddles and humour.
A gentle-man in every way, we think of him every day.
And to all the little bees that do such a great job in our gardens and fields.
– Craig Smith & Maureen Thomson

To Clarki~pooh ... endless gratty-chewed for your magical input,
inspiration and endless tiddlypoms
– Katz Cowley

First published in 2010 by Scholastic New Zealand Limited
Private Bag 94407, Botany, Manukau 2163, New Zealand

Scholastic Australia Pty Limited
PO Box 579, Gosford, NSW 2250, Australia

Text © Craig Smith & Maureen Thomson, 2007
Illustrations © Katz Cowley, 2010

ISBN 978-1-86943-943-9

National Library of New Zealand Cataloguing-in-Publication Data

Smith, Craig, 1972–
Willbee the Bumblebee / story by Craig Smith & Maureen Thomson ;
illustrated by Katz Cowley ; music by Craig Smith.
ISBN 978-1-86943-943-9
1. Children's songs—Texts. [1. Bumblebees—Songs and Music.
2. Songs.] I. Thomson, Maureen. II. Cowley, Katz. III. Title.
782.42083—dc 22

12 11 10 9 8 7 6 5 4 3 2 1   0 1 2 3 4 5 6 7 8 9 / 1

Illustrations created in watercolours and essence of rose petals

Publishing team: Diana Murray, Penny Scown and Annette Bisman
Design by Book Design Ltd, www.bookdesign.co.nz

Scholastic New Zealand's policy, in association with Tien Wah Press, is to use papers
that are renewable and made efficiently from wood grown in sustainable forests, so as to
minimise its environmental footprint.

Willbee, the bumblebee,
lives his life in your garden
so happily.

Up early in the morning
till the evening hour,
flying around
from flower to flower.

Now everybody knows, I suppose,
without bees in your garden, nothing grows.

They take the pollen to where it's supposed to be.

That's how nature works.

Good job, Willbee!

Now bumblebees,
from the day they are
born,

wear a black and yellow jersey
just to keep them
warm,

and Willbee's was special,

it was a
perfect fit,

'cause Willbee's mother
had knitted it.

Willbee was out one sunny day,

unknown to him his jersey had begun to fray,

and his jersey caught
where it was torn ...

right on the end of
a rose's thorn.

And as Willbee flew away, he did not stop,

his jersey unravelled
from the bottom to the top,

and when he realised this,
he lost his hum ...

He was showing
the whole garden
his bare bum!

Well, with no jersey,
and being late in the day,

Willbee was so cold
he couldn't fly away.

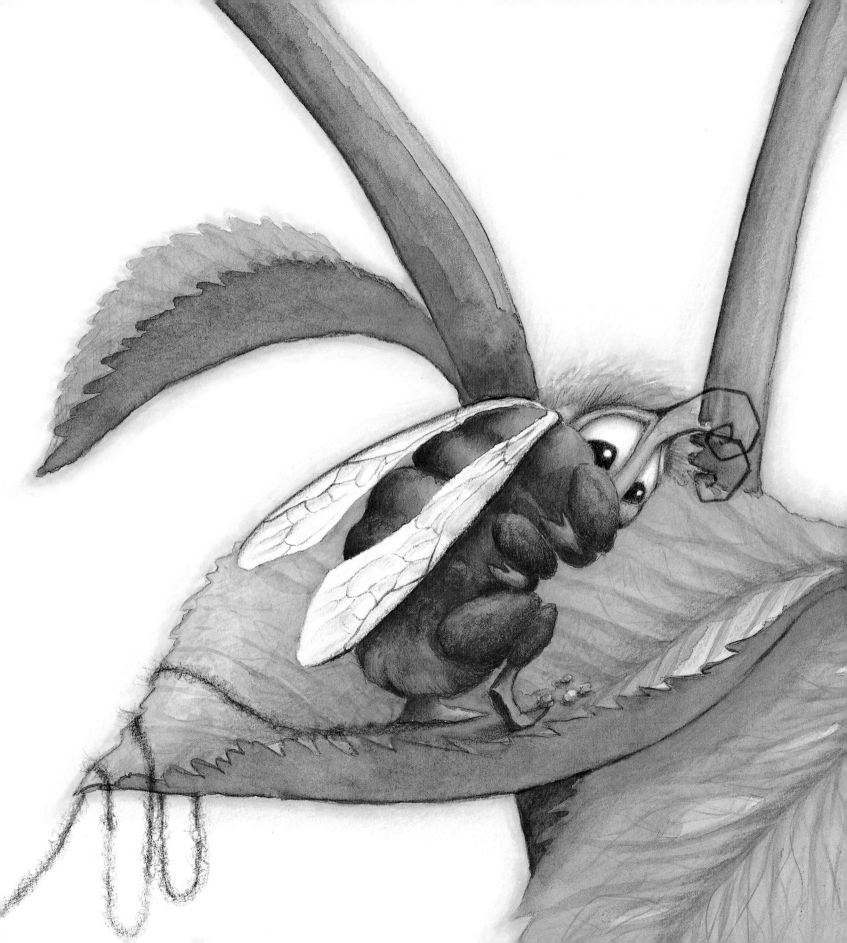

He was frightened,
and all alone.

All he wanted
to do was to
get home.

Now Monica the butterfly,
she flew down;

she told Willbee to
wipe off his frown.

She'd seen
what had happened
and thought she knew
what to do.

She gathered all the wool up,

and off she flew.

With the unravelled wool,
she flew to spider Steve
and asked him for help because she
knew he could weave.

With a twist of his arm,
she had him agree;
he would weave the wool they had
and make a new jersey.

Now spider Steve,
he finished so quickly!

He used a pattern
he'd found in the
Woman's Weekly.

Moni, with a smile,
　　she thanked him so,

　　but Willbee needed help
　　　　and now she had to go.

She found Willbee where he was last.

She said, "Quick! Put this on ...
really, really fast."

With his new jersey on,
he got back his
hum,

all his bits were warmed up ...
even his
bum!

Willbee hugged Moni
with a big thank you.

He asked her to thank
spider Steve for him too,

but now back to his house
he had to go,

for he knew his mum would worry
'cause she loved him so.

Now on a sunny day in your back yard,
you might still see Willbee, working hard,

from flower to flower, and carefree,
wearing his new
black and yellow jersey.